dick bruna

miffy
at the
seaside

EGMONT

Father Bunny said one day

who wants to come with me

down to the dunes and sandy beach

and then to see the sea?

Me, me, said Miffy, that is great

hurrah, I'll go as well

and I shall take my bucket too

in case I find some shells.

Right, said her dad, then in you get

I'm giving you a ride

we shall be at the beach quite soon

while you are safe inside.

Miffy went riding through the dunes

oh, aren't they high, she said

and Father Bun said, I can see

the beach there, straight ahead.

They stopped beside a jolly tent

look, Miff, we're here at last

you pulled so hard, cried little Miff

we travelled very fast.

Then Miffy took off all her clothes

and put her swimsuit on

well, well, said Father Bunny, that

was very quickly done.

So build a great big fortress now

here is your seaside spade

and I will make quite sure the fort

is well and strongly made.

Then Miffy dug with all her might

and built a solid wall

you see the top of Miffy's head –

the wall was very tall.

When Miff had finished digging

in all the yellow sand

she went to look for lovely shells

her bucket in her hand.

Then Father Bun took Miffy

to paddle in the sea

and Miffy splashed her daddy

as wet as wet can be.

As soon as they were dry again

said Dad, we cannot stay

it's time for home now, Miffy dear

it's been a lovely day.

That is a shame, cried Miffy

I'm not at all tired, but

once she was sitting in the truck

her eyes were soon tight shut.

miffy's library

miffy
miffy's dream
miffy's bicycle
miffy at the gallery
miffy at school
miffy at the playground

miffy in hospital
miffy at the zoo
miffy at the seaside
miffy the fairy
miffy's garden
miffy and the new baby

miffy is crying
miffy's birthday
miffy in the snow
miffy dances

"nijntje aan zee"
First published in Great Britain 1997 by Egmont UK Limited
239 Kensington High Street, London W8 6SA.
Publication licensed by Mercis Publishing bv, Amsterdam
Original text Dick Bruna © copyright Mercis Publishing bv, 1963
Illustrations Dick Bruna © copyright Mercis bv, 1963
Original English translation © copyright Patricia Crampton, 1996
The moral right of the author has been asserted.
Printed in Germany
ISBN 978 1 4052 0985 4
10 9
35300/9